Dedicated to my beloved father

The story of Gladys Thumpbucket originated when I was a small child. My dad would make up stories when he tucked me into bed, about this woman he liked called Mrs. Gladys Thumpbucket. He would mesmerise me with the tales and made me believe she was real. I was so engrossed with this woman and couldn't wait until bedtime.

After my dad passed away, it got me thinking and I thought about this character for so long about. I just wanted to bring her character to life through writing. My dad would say that Gladys was beautiful in her own way. She had straight hair, curly teeth, a cauliflower ear and a wonky eye and not forgetting her wooden leg!

So!! After all this time… this is for you dad. I would like to say a big thank you to you for all the wonderful childhood fantasies and memories. I hope that you're looking down on me, feeling proud and happy that finally! After all these years, I done something about it.

ACKNOWLEDGMENT

For many years… I've had this story of Gladys Thumpbucket in my imaginative mind. Never writing anything, just storing the adventures. The influence of the characters came from my Father.

The driving force came from my husband. He pushed me to gain the enthusiasm to eventually start this book and hopefully one of many.

I would like to say a huge thank you to Mr. Konrad Frazer-Kent! For believing in me and giving me the support and encouragement to get started. Finally I was able to take the time to actually sit down and write my first book.

Enjoy

Mrs Tracey A Frazer-Kent (Writer)

INTRODUCTION

In the heart of Wales stood a small beautiful village. Cottages were dotted around with a short walk to the neighbours' homes. The village was surrounded by steep mountains and green meadows. The scenery was breathe- taking and very peaceful.

In this particular village was this strange looking old lady, named Mrs. Gladys Thumpbucket!

You couldn't really describe her in only one word - there are several different unique features. This Lady was remarkable, friendly and clumsy in every way. She lived alone in this run-down old cottage with her black and white beloved cat Solomon. Her late husband Reg built Meadow Cottage many years ago.

The cottage was on its own on the top of a steep hill, with breath-taking views. It was quite shabby and so much needed doing around the place. The windows needed replacing. The bricks were starting to crumble around the building and the roof needed attention also. It would cost way too much money to re-do everything, so Gladys just put up with it.

Many years ago she had a skiing accident in the French Alps. Her left leg had to be removed and she makes do with a wooden peg leg, she does wobble a bit but she moves around ok.

Gladys was born with a few problems. Her right ear wouldn't form properly - it grew into a huge cauliflower shaped ear and sometimes she struggles to hear properly. Her teeth were never straight even when she had her milk teeth, they formed curly. Gladys's eyes were ok up until her teenage years, when one day she woke up with one of them wonky. So you can imagine this dear old lady doesn't have much luck in the looks department, but her character makes up for it.

Gladys was extremely clumsy, and accident prone was in her nature. She was terrible at doing anything without injuring herself, she would either bump into things or break stuff. Gladys was always apologising for her silly behaviour or being rather embarrassed. When she spoke to people, they roared with laughter at her little stories of chaos.

Gladys was a very slim girl in her childhood - now as an older lady she has somewhat gained a massive amount of weight. She has a big appetite and having a love for the sweet treats really doesn't help her much. Gladys finds it hard to move about quickly with the excess weight and her wooden leg. She is content with herself and it don't seem to bother her at all.

Gladys has a wonderful friend that lives nearby called Mr Dan. He is a very tall man and a kind individual. He ends up helping Gladys out of lots of sticky situations.

Mr. Dan also helps with her problems - which she does have lots of them also. In this book she has to rely on Mr. Dan once again.

Her trusted cat Solomon comes to the rescue and sets out on an adventure of his own.

Chaos happens in the furniture store and embarrassed faces are had by all.

The Shopping Trip

CONTENTS

- **Dedicated to**
- **Acknowledgment**
- **Introduction**
- **Contents**
- **Chapters**

THE ADVENTURES OF GLADYS THUMPBUCKET

The Shopping Trip

Chapter One

The birds were busy chirping away to each other in the distance, singing their early morning call. They were flying on and off the branches of the big oak trees, looking for food to eat.

The rubbish bin lorry was making its way into the lane and the bin men were making loud banging noises. Early morning workers were revving up their car engines nearby, getting ready for their long day at work. The lights outside started flickering as morning began to break.

The meadow cottage was fairly old and small. It had wooden floor boards that made such a creepy noise, especially when Gladys is stomping around with her wooden leg. It had wonky walls made out of red dusty brick. The ceilings were low with cracks starting to form in a line. Cobwebs were dangling from the corners of the room, with the odd ugly spider showing up unexpectedly. The roof was thatched and needed replacing as it was gathering small holes and getting a bit thread bare in places.

THE ADVENTURES OF GLADYS
THUMPBUCKET/Frazer-Kent

The cottage stood on its own with a very large garden. The view from there had beautiful meadows that were different shades of glorious green. High top mountains were surrounding it, which were incredible.

A few sheep were huddled together, sleeping and protecting themselves from the howling wind. The meadow also had one oversized friendly cow that liked his own company. He was always eating and he could never get enough food. He was very nosey and he would creep up to the fence to see what was going on.

A few deer sometimes came to visit, while out on their adventures. They would stop off to rest for a bit then they would move on to the next field.

There was an old tatty shed situated to left of the cottage, which had little mice visitors that liked to chew holes through the wood and make themselves quite at home. Huge cobwebs hung from the roof that had rather large spiders that also made this their home. The shed was so full to the brim, it was bulging at the sides - it had everything in there that you could possibly think of!

The scenery all around was simply breath taking, especially the mountains. When the cold winter came the mountain tops would glisten with snow. You could easily lose yourself dreaming, as it was so peaceful whilst staring off into the magical unknown.

THE ADVENTURES OF GLADYS THUMPBUCKET/Frazer-Kent

Mrs. Gladys Thumpbucket lived in this run-down cottage on her own with her cat Solomon. She would never move away from it as it held many a memory. Her heart was in the walls of the place and she loved it dearly. Gladys was not only born there but she also lived with her parents and her late husband Reg. She now lives alone and will stay there till her last breath. She had also collected so much clutter over the years that no removal men would want to take on that job should she ever want to move.

The attic was also extremely cluttered, with so much junk. It needed a really good sort through to get rid of all the things she no longer used. But Gladys just couldn't bring herself to go through all of her husband's belongings, even after all this time, so she just chucked it all up there out of the way for now.

The wind was still howling outside and whistling through the creeks in the rotten window panes, making such an awful sound. Damp was starting to creep in and there was a slight musty smell in each of the rooms.

This particular morning in Gladys's bedroom, she rudely awoke startled and gave an almighty shriek!

As she woke up, she swallowed a fly whilst opening her mouth to take a huge yawn and a massive stretch. Her wonky slatted eye opened up as wide as it could, looking confused. She wondered what on earth had happened... then her other eye flickered open.

THE ADVENTURES OF GLADYS THUMPBUCKET/Frazer-Kent

She stroked back her thin straight hair from her face, coughed out the fly and glanced down at the bottom of her bed.

'OH MY! What the devil have I done now? '

Gladys wasn't sure exactly what had happened whilst she was asleep… Perhaps she had a dream of digging a hole in the garden with her foot or maybe even dancing around a handbag at a disco? Whatever the dream, she somehow managed to get her wooden peg leg stuck through the bent slats in the bottom of her bed!

'How on earth will I get out of this mess by myself?'

Gladys said as she laid still for a few minutes in silence, to gather her thoughts. Talking away to herself she scratched her head thinking of all the possibilities that could free her leg. Without being able to sort the problem herself, she panicked and screamed out for help when she realised help was needed.

She knew she needed to think fast!!

'SOLOMON!' shouting out for her beloved feline. Solomon raised his weary head up from his curled-up body and feeling rather sleepy. He heard Gladys command coming from the bedroom.

'I need your help my love' Gladys shouted from upstairs. 'I'm going to have to rely on you to go and fetch help for me'.

THE ADVENTURES OF GLADYS THUMPBUCKET/Frazer-Kent

Solomon pounced up the stairs missing every other step and ran into the bedroom; He froze on the spot and was startled at the site of his precious owner. He jumped onto the mattress to give Gladys a lick on her face.

'Solomon... I do hope you can understand me, I want you to go to Mr. Dan's place down the lane and try your hardest to get him to come up here.' He peered up from licking her face and looked at Gladys confused.

Solomon purred as he watched Gladys in distress, 'I'm a cat and you know I don't understand human language, but!! I think I know what you're trying to say to me. I will make my way there and do my best for you. I have got eyes and can see that you will need a big strong man, to push your enormous bottom out of that broken bed'.

Solomon quickly jumped off the bed thinking to himself he could be her hero and save the day. But before he set off on his little journey, he just had to eat his fine cuisine of a tuna breakfast- of course nothing came before that, especially today when he needed his energy for the walk.

He licked his lips clean of every crumb of food to make sure he didn't miss one single bit. He took a little drink of milk from his bowl, then he ventured outside through the cat flap into the cold and windy morning.

THE ADVENTURES OF GLADYS THUMPBUCKET/Frazer-Kent

Chapter two

There were a lot of large dark rain clouds appearing as Solomon began to head off on his journey but it didn't bother him at all. He needed to do this regardless of the weather. Off he ran down the driveway on his mission with his head held high. After a few yards, Solomon stopped to have a quick wee and to have a little scratch under his left ear. That ear was always the itchiest place on his black and white fur and Solomon realised he wasn't as fit as he used to be.

The wind was starting to grow stronger and it almost blew Solomon off his feet! After catching his breath, he puffed out his chest and raised his little head to fight off the cruel wind. The sudden strong gusts kept moving him backward a few spaces so he puffed out his cheeks once more, took a big sniff and trotted off again.

A few yards away from Meadow Cottage, Solomon stepped into an open space of countryside. He felt so small amongst the massive surroundings that everything seemed enormous. The rain cloud broke and splatters started to leak from the sky, suddenly turning to big droplets and splashing onto his tiny little scrunched up nose making his eyes blurry.

Solomon walked a bit further and stepped onto the lane. He started running faster along the grey stoned path. He was making his way to Mr. Dan's cottage which was less than half a mile away.

THE ADVENTURES OF GLADYS THUMPBUCKET/Frazer-Kent

His paws were pounding down in the big circular puddles, making extra thuds and forming big exciting splashes. The downpour only lasted for a few minutes, giving way to bursts of sunshine sparkling through the clouds and the rain dried up just as quick as it had appeared.

Solomon stood still for a second so he could shake his furry wet coat from his head to his paws to get rid of the excess water.

At a nice steady pace, with the sun on his face he started to enjoy himself being free but knew he had an important task to do. He turned left and walked up to the next meadow.

Over in the field the big old cow approached to raise his lazy head and say good morning. Solomon looked up at him and gave him a meow.

In the distance he could make out Mr. Dan's place. It seemed so far to him as he only had little paws to get him there, but to humans it was only around a twenty-minute stroll.

The weather was changing all the time, it was now a beautiful bright blue sky up above and the clouds had all but disappeared. It was beginning to be a very pleasant day, except for the wind. The birds were still doing their thing, chirping away happily.

THE ADVENTURES OF GLADYS THUMPBUCKET/Frazer-Kent

Solomon stopped again to look down at the scurrying ants that were carrying their baggage, back and forth in a long line to find a safe place to hide their goods. Rabbits were jumping in and out of the holes in the meadow, minding their own business.

As he admired the views, Solomon slowed to a trot hoping to find more nibbles of food amongst the wildlife. He started feeling quite thirsty and hot, so he wandered off track to find a puddle of water that hadn't dried up. He came across one and took a big long drink.

He found some shelter under a tree that had fell down in the wind and curled up there for a few moments just to rest and cool of a little. He knew he couldn't stay there for long as Gladys was in trouble at home, so he started off on his way again.

Solomon climbed up the long drive to Mr. Dan's cottage huffing and puffing. He was now walking slowly up the gravel path because his paws were aching so much and his pads were very hot from the heat of the sun.

Feeling tired he collapsed a few yards away from the porch and slumped over the door mat. After taking a short snooze to re-charge himself, he dragged his body nearer. Looking up at the front door he gave his loudest meow, which by now took every bit of his strength.

Mr. Dan's place was a fairly large property that had lots of beautiful decorations, nothing like Gladys's place!

THE ADVENTURES OF GLADYS THUMPBUCKET/Frazer-Kent

He was quite good with his hands and enjoyed fixing things, also he liked to make lots of different pieces of furniture. He was also very neat and tidy - everything had its place and he knew where to find things easily.

After a few minutes of crying outside, (that seemed hours to poor Solomon) he now had a bit of a croak in his little voice. Finally the door flung open wide, with a huge bang. Mr. Dan came outside and took a look to see what all the noise was about. He was tall and thin with a very smart appearance and was always very polite. He bent over to stroke Solomon, with worry in his eyes.

'Hello my little furry friend! Why are you purring so loudly? Are you looking for scraps of food again?'

Solomon crept up towards him, stopped at Mr. Dan's huge size twelve feet and stared up at him with his big googly eyes. He tried to let him know that Gladys needed his help. How an earth was a scraggy little cat going to do that and get him to Meadow Cottage, to help poor old Gladys with her leg?

With a puzzled look on his face, Mr. Dan bent down and spoke to Solomon in a soft voice 'Well Solomon, this is very unlike you to travel this far and not beg me for any food. Something can't be right… maybe you're trying to tell me something?' Taking a deeper look at poor old Solomon, he decided that he needed to investigate this further.

THE ADVENTURES OF GLADYS
THUMPBUCKET/Frazer-Kent

He gave a big sigh, grabbed his coat and cap from the cloak stand and put on his big oversized boots then slammed the front door behind him.

Solomon was so relieved he gave out a loud piercing noise that echoed through the air. 'Thank goodness'! He thought as he managed to succeed in his first step of being a hero.

'Come on then my friend lets go and see what is bothering you.' Mr. Dan said to him.

So off they went up the lane. Mr. Dan was starting to panic a little, but he didn't let Solomon know this. Just as they approached the bottom of the drive the sky turned a horrible dark colour. The clouds started to form together again and it looked like it had turned into night all of a sudden. Mr. Dan looked down at Solomon.

'Looks like we are going to have heavy rain my little one, let's hurry along as we wouldn't want to get stuck in it'.

He started walking at a very fast pace and taking large steps whilst whistling away to himself. Poor old Solomon was struggling to catch up - he was so exhausted, he had to jump and stride a little quicker.

THE ADVENTURES OF GLADYS THUMPBUCKET/Frazer-Kent

They went past the meadow and all the animals were starting to take shelter ready for the downpour of rain once more. Even the nosey cow couldn't be bothered to lift his head up.

Solomon found some food amongst the weeds, so he stopped, nibbled and had a little drink of water from a huge leaf that had fallen to the ground.

Mr. Dan had not noticed Solomon had stopped so was now half a mile away. He suddenly turned around to find Solomon in the distance. He shouted to hurry him along. It was worth going that little bit faster – just as they approached Meadow Cottage, the heavens opened.

THE ADVENTURES OF GLADYS THUMPBUCKET/Frazer-Kent

Chapter 3

Mr. Dan bent down, grabbed the key from under the plant pot, and unlocked the door. He flung open the wooden front door, which was hanging on for dear life and crept inside. Solomon raced past him and dived up the stairs nearly tripping over his tail to investigate first.

It was weirdly quiet, just a little noise from the kitchen tap dripping.
'I must get that washer on thc tap sorted for Gladys' he said to himself. Mr. Dan would always pop over once a week to see if Gladys needed anything done. He liked to feel useful since his wife was no longer alive and he and Gladys had been friends for many years.

He followed Solomon up the steep old carpeted stairs to Gladys's bedroom.
'Gladys are you ok? It's Mr. Dan, can I come in to your bedroom? I'm not too sure what I'm doing here but! I'm sensing something isn't right as Solomon has paid me a visit...'
"GLADYS!" he shouted out, but there was just silence. He had no choice but to push the bedroom door, which was slightly opened as he feared she might be in big trouble.

THE ADVENTURES OF GLADYS THUMPBUCKET/Frazer-Kent

Gladys was led in the bed snoring away as loud as a freight train speeding along the rail track.

She really didn't look comfortable led in a ditch where the bed was broken! Her peg leg was wedged firmly beneath the bottom of the bed. The mattress had obviously moved slightly without her knowing. She managed to fall back to sleep while she was waiting of help. Mind you... Gladys could sleep standing up in the middle of a noisy supermarket!

Solomon jumped up onto the bed and scratched Gladys on her arm with his claw, making a noise next to Gladys's cauliflower ear. She shot upwards and squashed poor Solomon, lashed her arm out and knocked Mr. Dan's hat flying across the room!

'Yes, ok I'll have 2 jam donuts please!' she shouted out still half a sleep, then she glanced over at Mr. Dan.

'Oh dear I am terribly sorry, I must have been dreaming.'

Gladys apologised for the outburst and for knocking his hat off. She picked up her furry friend and stroked him.

'Thank you Solomon, you trusted little thing for bringing Mr. Dan here to help rescue silly ole me.'

THE ADVENTURES OF GLADYS THUMPBUCKET/Frazer-Kent

Mr. Dan replied 'no problem' and got onto his hands and knees to check out what had happened and how to fix it.

'Oh my! What have you done this time Gladys Thumpbucket?' He said with a huge grin on his face and a laughter in his voice.

'What an earth did you do to break this? This is your third new bed in less than two months.' Gladys does make a habit of breaking nearly everything - she is such a clumsy individual.

'Well I am not really sure to be honest with you. I seemed to have gained a few more pounds lately and I think maybe I'm getting a little bit heavy for this bed now. I must have had a stressful dream as I tossed and turned a lot. The bed must have snapped during the night without me knowing!'

The thing is Gladys is a large lady and her passion was to over indulge on gooey cakes. This didn't help as she couldn't do the simple things in life without getting out of breath because of her size.

Mr. Dan just smiled at her and got on with trying to get the problem fixed. He managed to loosen the bed slats first so he could free Gladys's wooden leg.

THE ADVENTURES OF GLADYS THUMPBUCKET/Frazer-Kent

'There you go Mrs Thumpbucket, how does that feel now?'

'WOW!! That's better! The feeling of being trapped was so frightening; God!! I feel like a prize idiot once again.' She said, knowing it won't be the last time she would be calling on Mr. Dan to rescue her.

'Right then let's get you up out of there so I can take this bed apart and take it outside.'

'Ok! Could you let me get dressed first, as I am not respectable at this present moment in time? Can you please pass me my dressing gown?'

Mr. Dan left the room to give Gladys her privacy. He went down stairs to wait in the kitchen so she could get her clothes on as she was still in her nightie and oversized big bloomers. Oh, what a sight it was! Gladys got herself ready and adjusted her peg leg, which was slightly off balance due to the upheaval of being pulled away from the mess she was in. Mr. Dan waited patiently with Solomon and made a cup of tea for them both. Gladys appeared in the kitchen doorway a few minutes later and gave him an awkward smile, showing off her curly teeth.

THE ADVENTURES OF GLADYS THUMPBUCKET/Frazer-Kent

'I'll finish my cuppa and I'll start taking your broken bed apart. I suppose we will have to go shopping to get you a new one.'

After drinking her tea and finishing breakfast, she went to get changed properly into outdoor clothes. The bed was all broken up outside by then. She grabbed her rain mac from the coat stand and put on her woolly hat. She found her one wellington boot that was shoved under the mess of shoes and slipped it on. Gladys picked up the truck keys and off they went outside to the garage.

The big garage was full to the brim with old house junk and rusty work tools. Amongst all the clutter stood her late husband's truck. It hardly ever got used, it was underneath a large sheet which she pulled off. After brushing the collected dust that had settled over time they both got in and sat comfortably.

Mr. Dan started the engine and it roared loudly, it blew out some old smoke from the exhaust and then they were all set to go.

THE ADVENTURES OF GLADYS
THUMPBUCKET/Frazer-Kent

It was still raining quite heavy and the windscreen
wipers of Gladys's old American truck were moving
rapidly. Steam appeared and misted the windows up
from Gladys's deep breathing.

Mr. Dan was insured to drive Gladys's truck as she could
no longer drive it with having a wooden leg.

Her late husband Reg had bought the vehicle years ago
but she couldn't bear to part with it. He spent many a
long day tinkering around the engine, cleaning and
polishing it.

She drove it for a short while before her major accident.
While she was skiing in the French Alps! She had a
horrible fall down one of the biggest slopes and drifted
into a nearby barb wired fence. The leg was so infected
they had to remove it. Adjusting to life with a wooden
leg was hard and driving was not an option anymore.

They left Solomon at home of course curled up under the
old oak tree in the garden. It was his favourite place after
all, plus it was very sheltered there and he wouldn't get
his shaggy fur wet. I think he was relieved to have some
peace, as he was so tired after his long journey.

THE ADVENTURES OF GLADYS THUMPBUCKET/Frazer-Kent

Chapter four

Off they drove to the big furniture store a few miles away, to replace yet another bed. They knew Gladys extremely well at the store as she has often visited the place to buy things she had broken.

On the way there they chatted and giggled as Gladys was a huge chatterbox and liked to talk a lot. Mr. Dan liked to listen to her! He could also chat just as much.

The journey there was slow as people were being careful because of the weather. The rain was slightly coming to a halt and the sky was trying its hardest to change colour into a light blue. The windscreen started drying up, and the wipers were now making a horrid squeaking noise.

Mr. Dan was driving at a nice steady pace along the country roads. They drove up to some steep humps in the road that were way too high.

'Up's daisy! Oh dearie me,' Gladys shouted out when they went over the speed bumps without slowing down enough. 'Oh, I'm so sorry Mr. Dan I have just let out a little puff of air from my bottom!'

THE ADVENTURES OF GLADYS THUMPBUCKET/Frazer-Kent

Mr. Dan looked sideways to look out the window to laugh as he couldn't control himself, he thought it was rather hysterical.

'That's ok Mrs. Thumpbucket you are amongst friends, these things are normal and do happen when you least expect it.'

'Well thank you my dear friend' with her face now a nice bright ruby colour. All the windows had to be opened, to let out the horrid whiff in the air!

They stopped at the traffic lights, just outside the parade of shops to wait for the lights to turn green. A huge black and white magpie must have been attracted to the whiff and pooped on the windscreen! Gladys put her hand to her head and saluted the dirty magpie out the way. As the old tale says... it's very bad luck and Gladys does not need any more of that.

They drove into the ever busy, overcrowded car park of the furniture store looking for a space big enough for their vehicle.

THE ADVENTURES OF GLADYS THUMPBUCKET/Frazer-Kent

Mr. Dan parked the old truck into a suitable space and switched of the engine. Gladys got out with a little help from Mr. Dan pushing from inside the car, to squeeze her large bottom out. She done a few neck stretches to straighten up her body and pulled down the back of her dress, which was slowly making its way up into her knickers.

They made their way through the double doors. Mr. Dan stopped to talk to Gladys, he leaned over and politely told her. 'Please! Let this be the last bed you have for a while.'

Gladys cleared her throat and looked him in the eye 'I will certainly do my best not to damage another one with this wooden peg leg again.'

THE ADVENTURES OF GLADYS THUMPBUCKET/Frazer-Kent

Chapter Five

The staff in the furniture store knew Gladys extremely well.

'Good afternoon Mrs. Thumpbucket! How can we help you today'? As Gladys approached the young lady.

'Well my dear! I have broken another bed, so I am here once again to hopefully buy another.'

Trying not to giggle, the young lady replied 'Ok no problem my dear, we can certainly try and help you with that. Why don't you have a look around first at the selection of beds we have? Then come and find me if you would like to try any out.'

Gladys replied rather embarrassed. 'Thank you! I will have a little peek and see what tickles my fancy.' Gladys then looked at Mr Dan, with a "here we go again" look and strolled off with a step and a thump.

There were lots of different beds to choose from that were spread out through the store and others that were on a second floor. Some obviously weren't very suitable for Gladys's needs as she suffers terribly with arthritis in her back so she needed a mattress that was firm and supporting.

THE ADVENTURES OF GLADYS THUMPBUCKET/Frazer-Kent

Not a big, super soft one that she could lose herself in and struggle to pull herself up on. That would just cause a lot more problems, especially knowing what sort of person Gladys is like.

There was a beautiful bed tucked away in the corner of the store that she liked, which was in her price budget. She walked over to the luxury bed and sat on the edge of the mattress. As she moved slightly the bed wobbled a bit and suddenly Gladys flew backwards on to the bed. Her legs shot up in the air, showing off her crisp white bloomers. Mr. Dan had to quickly look the other way, whilst offering his arm to help silly old Gladys up.

'No! I don't think I will be getting this one, she chuckled. 'Can you imagine me all the time getting into bed? I'd be doing acrobatics every night!'

The store was fairly busy with lots of people wandering and minding their own business. Gladys and Mr. Dan walked around looking at all the beds until they came across one that looked suitable.

Gladys put her hand on the bed first to test the firmness of it. 'Oh! I like this one, it says here on the label that it's very good for people who suffer with a bad back.'

THE ADVENTURES OF GLADYS THUMPBUCKET/Frazer-Kent

She took a look at the price tag first, her eyes opened wide and she nearly choked. She started to cough and splutter very loudly.

'I don't think I will be buying this one, I would need to sell my arm AND my wooden leg for that price!'

Gladys started feeling tired, wondering if she will be able to find a bed today. She called the store assistant over when one particular bed she saw looked interesting. 'Is it ok if I try that bed over there?' pointing over to the right side of the shop. 'It does look rather comfy!' The assistant looked puzzled,

'I'm afraid Mrs. Thumpbucket! That one is a luxury top of the range water bed, I'm not sure that would be suitable for you.'

But Gladys took a shine to it...

'I don't know, I rather fancy a water bed with the feeling of being on a boat on the deep blue sea.' With a little giggle she walked over to it excited. Mr. Dan looked at her and froze with panic as alarm bells started to ring in his head.

THE ADVENTURES OF GLADYS THUMPBUCKET/Frazer-Kent

Gladys was helped on to the bed by two of the assistants as it was fairly high to climb on to. She led down and got herself comfy.

'This feels wonderful' she squished herself from side to side, wriggling around like a worm. Another couple of store assistants appeared, they were looking straight at her with horror on their faces.

There were several people that were nearby looking for beds but even they had to stop and stare. Gladys bounced up and down like a child enjoying the feeling it made when it moved. The mattress started making an unusual sound and then the almighty happened… Her wooden leg got caught! She must have chipped some wood off from her broken bed and splinters were sticking right out.

'HELP ME!!' she screamed. 'I seem to have snagged the bed and I do believe I'm seriously stuck! Oh my goodness what have I done'.

She shouted out, apologising to everyone and kept on repeating herself. Her face went white as a sheet, her hands started shaking and she felt very sorry for herself. After a few more terrifying moments, Gladys started to calm down a little and felt slightly less embarrassed.

THE ADVENTURES OF GLADYS THUMPBUCKET/Frazer-Kent

She placed her hand underneath herself to try and lift her big bottom up. When she pulled her hand away it was soaking wet and so were her clothes!

'I'm not too sure what's happening down there, I have either wet my bloomers, or this bed is leaking!!' With confusion spread across her face. The other store assistants rushed over to help her immediately.

They managed to get her up off the bed, so they could see the damage she had done. One assistant grabbed hold of one arm and one grabbed the other.

Mr. Dan just stood there on the spot not knowing whether to laugh or cry, looking at Gladys in amazement.

After getting Gladys up to a sitting position, she then wiggled herself to the edge of the bed. As she stood up the room started spinning and dizziness came over her that made her sway side to side. All of sudden she tripped and fell over the store assistant's foot. Gladys was now in the air flying across the room at full speed, knocking all the lamps and vases off the shelves smashing them into small pieces. She landed on the floor with the loudest thud you could imagine.

THE ADVENTURES OF GLADYS THUMPBUCKET/Frazer-Kent

By now she could hear raised voices and laughter coming from behind her. Not wanting to turn around and face anyone just yet, she just looked down at the mess she had made on the floor.

Water was pumping out of the bed, going everywhere and running all over the showroom floor!

Pound signs flashed before her eyes and the thought of all the money she was going to spend was going through her mind, thinking of how much damage this shopping trip was going to cost her.

Not to mention of course, the embarrassment she has caused herself and Mr. Dan.

Mrs. "Accident prone" was her middle name, she really shouldn't ever leave the comfort of her house, she was thinking to herself. As she slowly got herself off the floor with a little help, she stood up with her head hung low and her wonky eye shut.

Her feet splashed in a pool of water as she slowly looked around at everyone. They were all in a state of shock at the horror that was going on in front of their eyes. She looked over at the bed, which had now shrunk into a squashed mess. Water was everywhere, and starting to flood the store - getting higher by the minute.

THE ADVENTURES OF GLADYS THUMPBUCKET/Frazer-Kent

Most of the people inside were running and wading out the door in a hurry. Some were falling over in the water and some were swimming to the entrance.

'Fiddle sticks this is a nightmare', Gladys said to Mr. Dan as soon as she noticed he too had fallen over into the stream of water that was running past him.

A few of the adults started panicking but the children loved it. They thought it was the best day ever! A few volunteers offered to help clear up the place by sweeping the pools of water outside with brushes and mops, but everything was starting to get ruined.

Mr. Dan grabbed hold of Gladys's arm before she fell over again and led her to the big open doorway of the store. He apologised for her as she was unable to speak through such embarrassment (it's not very often she is silent). 'We will of course pay for all the damage, but for now I do need to get Mrs. Thumpbucket home immediately. I do believe that she has had enough for one day'.

Everybody couldn't stop staring at them, with shocked expressions on their faces. They waved at them both awkwardly, completely speechless.

THE ADVENTURES OF GLADYS THUMPBUCKET/Frazer-Kent

Chapter 7

Gladys wobbled over to the truck hanging her head down in shame. She got in the truck and slumped down onto the seat.

'Well!! That was certainly an experience I wouldn't like to go through again'. Gladys let out a little whimper with a low croaky voice. 'I am so ashamed of myself; I'm feeling rather silly right now.'

Mr. Dan shook his head and fumbled around in his pocket for his keys and started up the engine.

'Let's get you home and settled and try not to worry about it for now. I'm sure it will all blow over and be forgotten about in a few days.'

He wasn't sounding very convincing - his voice said it all. Gladys looked out the window, watching other people getting in their cars. He pulled out of the car park in such a hurry, 'I'm positive that we will not be visiting that store again'.

Whilst driving along in the traffic he had an idea that he maybe should have thought about earlier.

THE ADVENTURES OF GLADYS THUMPBUCKET/Frazer-Kent

'Gladys! I've been thinking about your bed situation, I do believe that I might have a solution to the problem and I might be able to help you.'

'I'm positive I have an old sturdy bed at home in the garage that I was going to throw out some time ago. I'm almost certain it is still in there covered with a blanket. Let's go back to my place first and take a look shall we?'

'That sounds like a good plan to me,' Gladys whispered back to him.

The journey back was a little quiet, both pretty exhausted and still in a state of shock. All of a sudden a roar of laughter came out of Mr. Dan's mouth.

'Oh! Gladys you do make me smile!! I never know what can happen next with you and what fun adventures we are going to have. You're always surprising me with your unusual antics.' Gladys raised her eyebrows and showed off her curly teeth with a big open smile.

'I certainly know how to make a fool of myself in public don't I?' Gladys said sheepishly.

Mr. Dan spoke back softly. 'Well without sounding rude and being your friend of course, I think I'm able to comment on this.

THE ADVENTURES OF GLADYS THUMPBUCKET/Frazer-Kent

Yes you do! But it's never a dull moment that's for sure and what else can I do to get entertainment.'

While they were driving home Gladys sat back in her seat silently thinking of all the strange memories they've had during their friendship.

They pulled up on to the driveway at Mr. Dan's cottage and parked the old truck. He wandered over to the garage and started looking through all the mess. This was the only part of his home that was untidy.

Coming across the blanket he had in his mind, he pushed the old thing to one side and underneath was the bed he had remembered!

There was nothing wrong with it at all - it had been stuck in the garage for quite some time. It was he and his wife's first bed they had bought together many years ago. Gladys took a look - it was perfect for her.

'Why didn't I think of this much earlier, it would have saved all of that chaos and embarrassment …'What do you think? He went on 'It just needs a good airing and a wash down, then it will be like brand new. I can lift it out and put it on the back of the truck and take it to yours? We can leave it on the grass for a few hours to get the damp smell and dust off.'

THE ADVENTURES OF GLADYS THUMPBUCKET/Frazer-Kent

'Yes! Let's do that thank you once again, you're truly a remarkable friend and I really don't know what I would do without you.' Mr. Dan always got embarrassed with signs of affection but he secretly liked it.

He grabbed hold of the bed frame and placed it onto the back of the truck, followed by the mattress. It wasn't too heavy for him, just as well as he is not as fit as he used to be.

Driving up and down the winding lanes to Meadow Cottage (being careful not to hit any bumps as the bed wasn't very secure on the back), they finally arrived and pulled up on to the drive.

Solomon heard the truck door bang shut and peered up from his nap. Walking over to greet them, he thought to himself, "hurray… it could well be dinner time.' Always thinking of his belly as usual, just like his dear owner. He got up close to them, had a little scratch then purred out loud for a belly tickle. Mr. Dan got down on one knee, placed his giant hand on Solomon's belly and rubbed away.

He lifted the bed off and placed it on the grass near the cottage, in the full sun.

THE ADVENTURES OF GLADYS THUMPBUCKET/Frazer-Kent

Gladys went in doors to fetch the hoover and cleaning things. She got the hoover out, plugged it in and got ready to clean away the dust.

Mr. Dan gave her an awkward look.

'Gladys!! Step away from the machine, I will do it for you just in case we have any more accidents' tutting away. 'Why don't you go inside and make a cup of tea and cut us a huge slice of your cake for us both?'

'Yes! Ok your right, what a good idea it's probably for the best that I don't touch anything for the rest of the day. I'll get straight on to it.'

He gave the mattress a good hoover, a thorough wash down and left it to dry nicely in the sun.

'The bed is looking as good as new Gladys and hopefully it will stay that way. What a lovely sponge cake you've made, with lots of fresh cream and strawberry jam. Yummy!!

He washed the cake down with his strong cup of tea. 'Right! This won't do, it's starting to get late and I need the light to get that bed up your stairs.'

THE ADVENTURES OF GLADYS THUMPBUCKET/Frazer-Kent

He put his plate and cup in the kitchen and got his tools out of the truck to take the legs off the frame. With his screwdriver in his hand, he carefully loosened the screws. Solomon walked up to him with curiosity and sat right in front of him.

'Solomon!! Its dinner time' Gladys shouted out to him. It took two seconds to leap up and dash inside for his feast. While he was munching on his delight, Gladys was looking down at him with affection.

'You're about the only one that doesn't know how clumsy I am.' He wasn't taking any notice of her, just focused on his food bowl.

Mr. Dan went up and down the stairs with the legs, then followed by the frame. He set it all out ready in her bedroom to put it back together. Scratching his head under his cap, taking a few moments to think, he suddenly remembered that he had a headboard at home. He ran down the stairs as it was getting late, nearly tripping over the worn bit of carpet at the bottom.

'I'll be back in a bit, I've forgotten the headboard' and off he went.

Gladys was in the kitchen looking out the window and glaring across the meadow.

THE ADVENTURES OF GLADYS THUMPBUCKET/Frazer-Kent

The sun was starting to fade and the sky started to go dim. The wind was now calm and the birds were silent.

Mr. Dan was only gone fifteen minutes and she could hear the sound of the truck once more. He came bolting into the kitchen out of breathe and then went straight upstairs to start putting it all together. Whilst he was taking care of that, Gladys was sorting the bedding out ready to go on.

'Right Mrs.!! This better last you a bit longer than most of your beds. I think before I leave I shall smooth off your leg a bit. I'll go and get the sander from your shed, if that's ok? Said Mr. Dan. 'We need to take off some of those splinters sticking out as we don't want a repeat performance of today, I don't think my heart could handle anymore right now.'

He went down the garden to the shed, fighting his way through the large cobwebs and the incredibly big spiders, which didn't bother him at all. He grabbed the sander and headed back. Gladys sat down on the kitchen stool ready for him. Mr. Dan got settled next to her and got down to work, he made a few sweeping motions up and down the leg until it started to feel smooth.

'How does that feel? Any better?'

THE ADVENTURES OF GLADYS THUMPBUCKET/Frazer-Kent

'That is fine, if you took any more off it would look like a stick', she giggled loudly.

It was now getting dark outside and both of them were feeling very tired. He cleaned up the mess he had made, put on his coat and cap and said his goodbyes. Solomon looked up at him and gave him a stare. Gladys couldn't thank him enough.

'Hope you get a good night sleep tonight, try not to fidget too much' he giggled.

Gladys just laughed at him.

'I will have to strap my whole body down just in case I move a little.'

Mr. Dan stepped outside into the darkness of the night. Up above the stars were twinkling and the moon began to shine bright. He thought to himself 'I could do with a large brandy and an early night - tomorrow is another day'.

After Gladys waved at him goodbye she went up into the bedroom to make up her bed. She was hoping she would get wonderful sleep, which was very much needed.

THE ADVENTURES OF GLADYS THUMPBUCKET/Frazer-Kent

'All done Solomon, what do you think of this bed?'
Solomon had big stretch and leaped onto the bed to test
it out. Gladys changed into her nightie and dressing
gown and went back down to the kitchen. She poured
herself a night cap of sweet brandy and grabbing the
glass in her hand, she wondered off into the living room.

Falling into her beloved rocking chair, she got her
bottom comfy and relaxed. She pulled the knitted
blanket up around her and sat there rocking herself back
and forth. She took a huge sip from her brandy glass and
let out a big sigh.

'Gladys! You are a walking catastrophe, you really need
to think before you do things.'

She gave herself a right telling off and thought about the
phone call she would have to make to the store in the
morning, hoping they would go easy on her and be
polite.

Right now all she could do was rest and enjoy her drink
next to the open fire, which was making the room glow
nicely.

Solomon curled up on the soft rug right next to the fire
getting himself nice and warm.

THE ADVENTURES OF GLADYS
THUMPBUCKET/Frazer-Kent

Her eyes were drifting and her head was getting heavy, she got up from the chair and wandered upstairs.

Humming away while she was brushing her curly teeth, she wiped her face clean and turned off the bathroom light.

Getting into bed was a wonderful feeling, having nice fresh crisp sheets on and a heavy quilt. Solomon was already on the mattress getting ready to sleep, yawning away.

She led back on the bed exhausted and got into a comfy position. Slowly closing her eyes and hoping for pleasant dreams. She switched the lamp off, prayed that she would stay still and not have any problems while she was asleep this time.

Printed in Great Britain
by Amazon